DOG ON A LOG®
Get Ready! Readers (Blue)
Letter Group 2

I am not a Reading Specialist or certified educator, but I do have a lot of experience teaching my daughter with dyslexia how to read. At times, it was difficult to determine what to do and how to do it. It is my hope that the information provided within this book will make the journey a bit easier for other parents. The content provided herein is for informational purposes and does not take the place of an evaluation and teaching plan provided by a credentialed educator. Every effort has been made to ensure that the content provided here is accurate and helpful for my readers. However, this is not an exhaustive treatment of the subject. No liability is assumed for losses or damages due to the information provided. You should consult a credentialed educator for specific guidance on educating your child, yourself, or others.

DOG ON A LOG Books
Tucson, Arizona

TAG
(CLASSROOM AND HOME)
DOG ON A LOG (Blue) Get Ready! Readers 2

Letter Group 2
Companion to
THE SQUIGGLE CODE
(LETTERS MAKE WORDS)

By Pamela Brookes

Edited by Nancy Mather PhD

Table of Contents

For Parents and Teachers,

This book was created for schools. Some will use in it in their classrooms, others will provide it for reading practice at home. It is a single-story companion book to *THE SQUIGGLE CODE (LETTERS MAKE WORDS.)* Unlike *Kids' Squiggles*, this book contains just the Letter Group 2 story. It also contains words, sentences, and tracing letters from the book *The Squiggle Code*.

Some families may use it in addition to their school's reading instruction or as independent homeschoolers. Other families may prefer to use the more economical *Kids' Squiggles* and supplement the stories with the printable words and sentences from www.dogonalogbooks.com.

Scientific research has shown that the best way to learn to read is by using phonics.[1] This book is a beginning decodable reader. Like all DOG ON A LOG Books, it was written in a stairstep manner. Your child should master each Step of letters or phonics rules before they move on to the next Step. This gradual progression will allow your child to learn to read one Step at a time.

---

[1] *Put Reading First*, Third Edition, Center for the Improvement of Early Reading Achievement (CIERA) and funded by the National Institute for Literacy (NIFL)
https://lincs.ed.gov/publications/pdf/PRFbooklet.pdf

How to Use this Book

Your child's teacher will instruct them in the sounds to make for each letter. They will also teach them how to blend the letters into words and how to read the "sight words." To practice at home, you can ask your child to read the words, sentences, and story in the book. If they are having a hard time, help them make the sound of each letter while tapping their fingers (see next page on how to "tap.") Have your child make the sound of each letter, then ask them to say them as quickly as they can until they make each word. Some kids will do this right away, other kids may need lots of repetition.

A Note about Pictures

The pictures are included to break up the reading. Even a four-word sentence can be a lot for a new reader, especially if the child finds reading hard. However, do not ask your child to guess what the word is based on the picture. That does not teach kids how to sound-out and read words, it teaches them to guess. If your child is distracted by the picture, you may want to cover it with a sheet of paper. When the child successfully decodes (sounds-out) the sentence, then you can pull away the paper and get the reward of seeing the picture.

Tapping

Tapping is one of the most useful skills a new reader can learn. Now that their teacher has taught them to sound out words, you can ask them to "tap" a finger to their thumb for each sound in a word. It is harder to lose track of the letters if you are tapping your fingers for each sound. Have your child tap their thumb to their finger for each sound in the words. The pictures below show which finger to tap for each sound in the word. When they start tapping words with four sounds, they will tap the pinkie. For longer words they tap through the pinkie then start over with the pointer finger.

TAPPING:
First
sound
in a
word

TAPPING:
Second
sound
in a
word

TAPPING:
Third
sound
in a
word

Letter Group 2

r, d, c, g

Sight Words Introduced:
a, and, to, has

Letters Learned in Book 1

a, f, m, n, s, t

<u>r</u>at

r

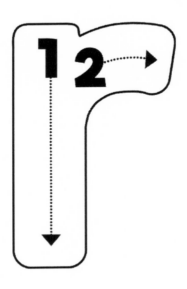

Rr

Capital R

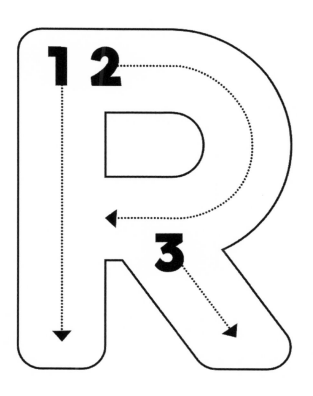

<u>d</u>og

d

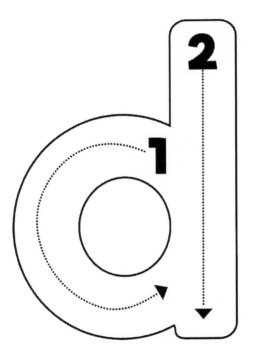

Dd

Capital D

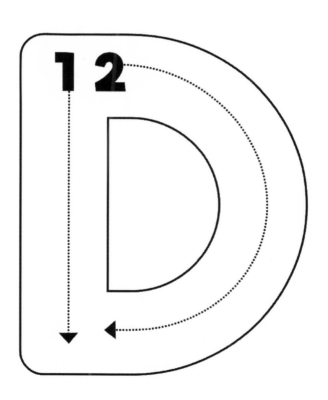

<u>c</u>at

C

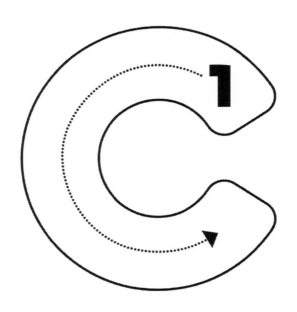

Cc

Capital C

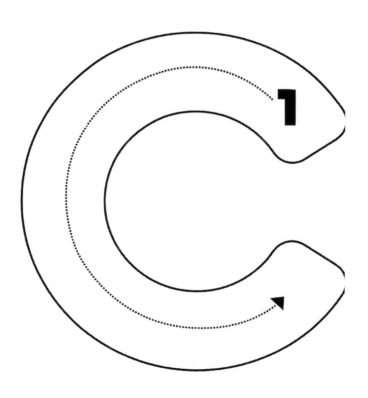

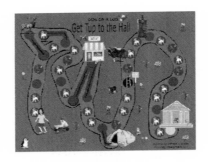

game

g

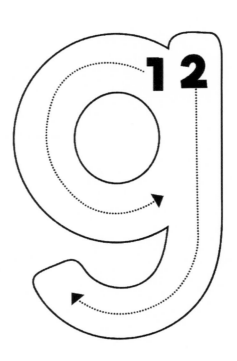

Gg

Capital G

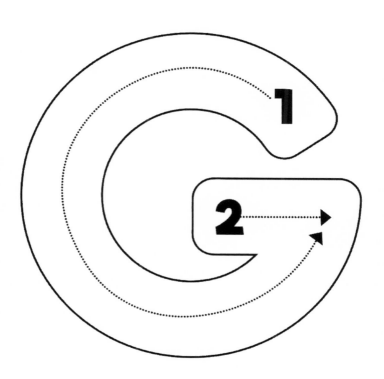

Words

ram	rat	ran
tag	sag	cat
can	gas	fad
Dan	Tad	Dad

Here are some silly words your child can sound out. Sounding out silly words is a good skill because it means they are not guessing.

gat	nad	cag

Sentence Time

1. Dan has a mat and a can.

2. Dad is sad and Dan is mad.

3. Sam the rat ran to Dan.

4. Tam the cat ran.

5.Can Dan tag Tad and Dad?

6.Tad the tan ram ran to Tam.

7.The sad rat has gas.

8.Tad the ram ran to the dam.

Story Time

Tag

New Sight Words:
a, and, to, has

Sight Words from Book 1:
is, the

Dan has a cat.

The cat is Tam.

Tam the cat ran to tag Dan.

Dan ran to tag Tad.

Tad is a ram.

Tad the ram ran to tag Dad.

Dad ran.

Dan ran to tag Tam the cat.

Tam the cat ran and ran.

Time to Rhyme Game

Let's make rhymes by changing the first letter of the following words.

Read this word:

tag

Let's change the first letter to "r."

Read this word:

rag

Let's change the first letter to "s."

Read this word:

sag

You can use magnetic letters or letter flashcards to play this game. Create silly words or real words. Just use the letters from Letter Groups 1 and 2.

Switch the End Game

What happens if we change the last letter?

Read this word:

ram

Let's change the last letter to "t."

Read this word:

rat

Let's change the last letter to "g."

Read this word:

rag

You can use magnetic letters or letter flashcards to play this game. Create silly words or real words. Just use the letters from Letter Groups 1 and 2.

D'Nealian Letters
for Tracing

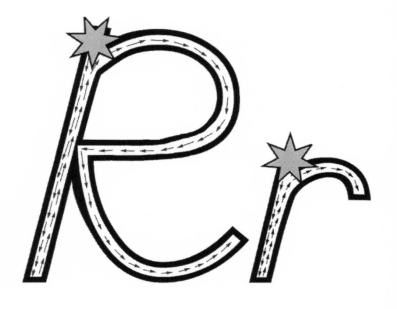

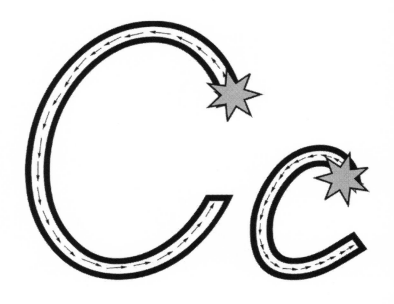

Download DOG ON A LOG printable gameboards, games, flashcards, and other activities at www.dogonalogbooks.com/printables.

Parents and teachers: If you would like to receive email notifications of new DOG ON A LOG Books and/or printables, please subscribe to our email notification list: www.dogonalogbooks.com/subscribe

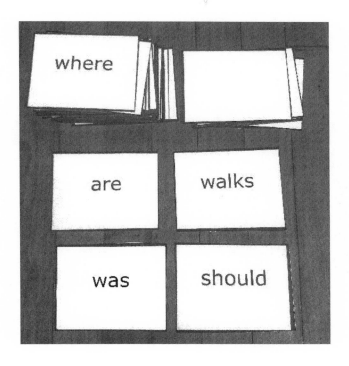

Keywords

Alphabet

Aa	Bb
apple	bat
Cc	Dd
cat	dog

Ee	Ff
Ed	fun
Gg	Hh
game	hat
Ii	Jj
itch	jug

Kk	Ll
<u>k</u>ite	<u>l</u>amp
Mm	Nn
<u>m</u>an	<u>n</u>ut
Oo	Pp
<u>o</u>ctopus	<u>p</u>an

Qu qu	Rr
queen	rat
Ss	Tt
snake	top
Uu	Vv
up	van

Ww	Xx
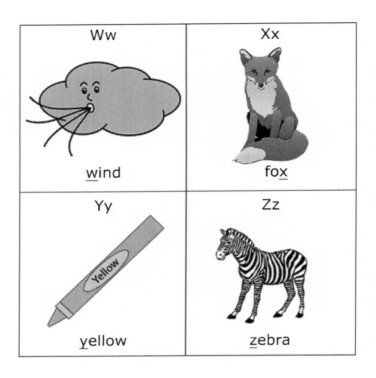 wind	fo<u>x</u>
Yy	Zz
<u>y</u>ellow	<u>z</u>ebra

DOG ON A LOG Books
Phonics Progression

DOG ON A LOG Get Ready! Books
Book 1
Phonological/Phonemic Awareness
- Words
- Rhyming
- Syllables, identification, blending, segmenting
- Identifying individual letter sounds

Books 2-3
Phonemic Awareness/Phonics
- Consonants, primary sounds
- Short vowels
- Blending
- Introduction to sight words

DOG ON A LOG
Get Ready! Readers 1 to 7 (Blue)
Classroom & Home alternative to Get Ready! Book 3

Books 1-7
Phonemic Awareness/Phonics
- Consonants, primary sounds
- Short vowels
- Blending
- Introduction to sight words

DOG ON A LOG Get Set! Books
(3-letter word (cvc) books coming soon)

DOG ON A LOG Let's GO! and Chapter Books

Step 1
- Consonants, primary sounds
- Short vowels
- Digraphs: ch, sh, th, wh, ck
- 2 and 3 sound words
- 's (Possessive s)
- Closed syllables

Step 2
- Bonus letters (f, l, s, z after short vowel)
- "all"
- –s suffix

Step 3
- Letter buddies: ang, ing, ong, ung, ank, ink, onk, unk

Step 4
- Consonant blends to make 4 sound words
- 3 and 4 sound words ending in –lk, -sk

Step 5
- Digraph blend –nch to make 3 and 4 sound words
- Silent e, including "-ke" (vce syllables)

Step 6

- Exception words containing: ild, old, olt, ind, ost

Step 7

- 5 sounds in a closed syllable word plus suffix -s (crunch, slumps)
- 3 letter blends and up to 6 sounds in a closed syllable word (script, spring)

Step 8

- Two-syllable words with 2 closed syllables, not blends (sunset, chicken, unlock)

Step 9

- Two-syllable words with all previously introduced sounds including blends, exception words, and silent "e" (blacksmith, kindness, inside)
- Double vowel syllables
- Vowel digraphs: ai, ay, ea, ee, ie, oa, oe (rain, play, beach, tree, pie, boat, toe)

Step 10

- Open syllables (be, so, hi)
- "Y" as a vowel with the long "I" sound in open syllables (my, spry)
- Two-syllable words containing:
  - Open syllables (beside, rerun)
  - Vowel teams ai, ay, ea, ee, ie, oa, oe (raindrop, teacup)
  - Previously learned sight words (somewhere, friendship)

Step 11

- R-controlled syllables ar, er, ir, or,
  ur (star, fern, bird, fork, surf)
- One-syllable words with -ire (tire)
- Three-syllable words with known
  phonics and sight words
  (chimpanzee, Wyoming, waterway)

WATCH FOR MORE STEPS COMING SOON
See www.dogonalogbooks.com for a
complete list

**Let's GO! Books
have less text**

**Chapter Books
are longer**

DOG ON A LOG Books
Sight Word Progression

DOG ON A LOG Get Ready! Books and Get Ready! Readers
a, does, go, has, her, is, of, says, the, to

DOG ON A LOG Let's GO! and Chapter Books

Step 1
a, and, are, be, does, go, goes, has, he, her, his, into, is, like, my, of, OK, says, see, she, the, they, to, want, you

Step 2
could, do, eggs, for, from, have, here, I, likes, me, nest, onto, or, puts, said, say, sees, should, wants, was, we, what, would, your

Step 3
as, Mr., Mrs., no, put, their, there, where

Step 4
push, saw

Step 5
come, comes, egg, pull, pulls, talk, walk, walks

Step 6
Ms., so, some, talks

Step 7
Hmmm, our, out, Pop E., TV

Step 8
Dr., friend, full, hi, island, people, please

Step 9
about, aunt, cousin, cousins, down, friends, hi, inn, know, knows, me, one, ones, TVs, two, water, welcome

Step 10
because, been, coyote, coyote's, coyotes, door, four, grosbeak, grosbeak's, grosbeaks, javelina, laugh, laughs, many, more, only, uh, very, were, who, word, words, x-ray

WATCH FOR MORE BOOKS COMING SOON
  See www.dogonalogbooks.com for a
  complete list

More DOG ON A LOG Books

Most books available in Paperback, Hardback, and
e-book formats

DOG ON A LOG Parent and Teacher Guides

Book 1 (Also in FREE e-book and PDF Bookfold)
- Teaching a Struggling Reader: One Mom's Experience with Dyslexia

Book 2 (FREE e-book and PDF Bookfold only)
- How to Use Decodable Books to Teach Reading

DOG ON A LOG Get Ready! Books

Book 1 (Get Ready! Guide 1)
- Before the Squiggle Code (A Roadmap to Reading)

Book 2 (Get Ready! Guide 2)
- The Squiggle Code (Letters Make Words)

Book 3 (Seven stories from Book 2)
- Kids' Squiggles (Letters Make Words)

DOG ON A LOG
Get Ready! Readers 1 to 7 (Blue)
Classroom & Home alternative to
Get Ready! Book 3
(Words, Sentences and Stories from Get Ready! Books 2 & 3)

- Nan Fam (Letters a, s, m, f, t, n)
- Tag (Adds letters r, d, c, g)
- The Tot (Adds letter o)
- Max and Sal (Adds letters b, h, l, x)
- Bip, Sop, Lob (Adds letters i, p, k, j)
- Jan and Quin (Adds letters u, y, z, qu)
- Wet Van (Adds letters e, v, w)

DOG ON A LOG Get Set! Books
(3-letter word (cvc) books coming soon)

DOG ON A LOG Let's GO! and Chapter Books

All titles starting with Step 1 can be purchased as red chapter books. They are available individually or with all the same-step books in one volume.

Steps 1-5 titles can be bought as purple Let's GO! Books. They are shorter than the chapter books. They help some kids who feel intimidated by the longer chapter books.

Step 1
- The Dog on the Log
- The Pig Hat
- Chad the Cat
- Zip the Bug
- The Fish and the Pig

Step 2
- Mud on the Path
- The Red Hen
- The Hat and Bug Shop
- Babs the 'Bot
- The Cub

Step 3
- Mr. Bing has Hen Dots
- The Junk Lot Cat
- Bonk Punk Hot Rod
- The Ship with Wings
- The Sub in the Fish Tank

Step 4
- The Push Truck
- The Sand Hill
- Lil Tilt and Mr. Ling
- Musk Ox in the Tub
- The Trip to the Pond

Step 5
- Bake a Cake
- The Crane at the Cave
- Ride a Bike
- Crane or Crane?
- The Swing Gate

Step 6
- The Colt
- The Gold Bolt
- Hide in the Blinds
- The Stone Child
- Tolt the Kind Cat

Step 7
- Quest for A Grump Grunt
- The Blimp
- The Spring in the Lane
- Stamp for a Note
- Stripes and Splats

Step 8
- Anvil and Magnet
- The Mascot
- Kevin's Rabbit Hole
- The Humbug Vet and Medic Shop
- Chickens in the Attic

Step 9

- Trip to Cactus Gulch 1: The Step-Up Team
- Trip to Cactus Gulch 2: Into the Mineshaft
- Play the Bagpipes
- The Hidden Tale 1: The Lost Snapshot

Step 10

- The Chicken Bus Express to the Redo Shop
- The Rewind Clock: The Tale Begins
- Trip to the Wildlife Rehab
- The Hidden Tale 2: The Secret Unfolds

WATCH FOR MORE BOOKS COMING SOON
See www.dogonalogbooks.com for a complete list

How You Can Help

Parents often worry that their child (or even adult learner) is not going to learn to read. Hearing other people's successes (especially when they struggled) can give worried parents or teachers hope. I would encourage you to share your experiences with products you've used by posting reviews at your favorite bookseller(s) stating how your child benefited from those books or materials (whether it was DOG ON A LOG Books or another book or product.) This will help other parents and teachers know which products they should consider using. More than that, hearing your successes could truly help another family feel hopeful. It's amazing that something as seemingly small as a review can ease someone's concerns.

DOG ON A LOG
Quick Assessment

Have your child read the following words. If they can't read every word in a Step, that is probably where in the series they should start. Some children may benefit starting at an earlier step to help them build confidence in their reading abilities.
Get a printable assessment sheet at:
www.dogonalogbooks.com/assessment-tool/

Step 1
fin, mash, sock, sub, cat, that, Dan's

Step 2
less, bats, tell, mall, chips, whiff, falls

Step 3
bangs, dank, honk, pings, chunk, sink, gong, rungs

Step 4
silk, fluff, smash, krill, drop, slim, whisk

Step 5
hunch, crate, rake, tote, inch, mote, lime

Step 6
child, molts, fold, hind, jolt, post, colds

Step 7
strive, scrape, splint, twists, crunch, prints, blend

Step 8
finish, denim, within, bathtub, sunset, medic, habit

Step 9
hundred, goldfinch, tree, wheat, inhale, play, Joe

Step 10
be, remake, spry, repeat, silo, sometime, pinwheel

Step 11
far, north, spire, turn, inhabit, calculate, Wyoming

WATCH FOR MORE STEPS COMING SOON
See www.dogonalogbooks.com for a complete list

Made in United States
Orlando, FL
03 February 2023

29470554R00045